SON OF DRACULA

Victor G Ambrus

Oxford University Press

Oxford Toronto Melbourne

THIS BOOK MAY IRRITATE YOUR EYES, BUT WILL NOT HARM YOUR CLOTHES!

BOING! BOING! BOING!

To Sándor

Oxford University Press, Walton Street, Oxford OX2 6DP

Oxford   New York   Toronto
Delhi   Bombay   Calcutta   Madras   Karachi
Petaling Jaya   Singapore   Hong Kong   Tokyo
Nairobi   Dar es Salaam   Cape Town
Melbourne   Auckland

and associated companies in
Berlin   Ibadan

Oxford is a trade mark of Oxford University Press

© Victor G Ambrus 1986
First published 1986
Reprinted 1987, 1988, 1989
First published in Paperback 1988
Reprinted 1989

British Library Cataloguing in Publication Data
Ambrus, Victor
Son of Dracula.
I. Title
823'.914[J]   PZ7
ISBN 0–19–279813–8 (Hardback)
ISBN 0–19–272191–7 (Paperback)

Typeset by Oxford Publishing Services
Printed in Hong Kong

Count Dracula was broke again. Nobody wanted to see his films any more, and his video nasties had all been pirated. The tourists had stopped visiting Castle Dracula and went to the Costa Packet instead.

The Count was forced to make a drastic decision – he had to marry a rich girl. In his newspaper he saw a photo of the chain-store heiress, Miss Tesco Smith-Spencer. He left for England at once.

As soon as they met, the beautiful heiress fell in love and they were married.

After a great society wedding, they flew to Transylvania where they lived happily for a while afterwards.

A year later – to Count Dracula, a son. His name was put down for Eton.

Drac Junior started school on Monday. After biting everyone in sight he was expelled on Saturday.

So Dracula decided to open his own school and call it Tombstoun.

Prospectuses were sent out with every issue of *Fox and Hound*, and soon large numbers of unwanted offspring were packed off to Transylvania.

When the young gentlemen arrived at Transylvania station, they thought it was jolly spiffing of the headmaster to meet them. It was even more spiffing to have a ride on the Tombstoun coach through the beautiful countryside to howls of approval from the onlookers.

They were all impressed by the tall, dark, handsome building and by the past pupils.

Mr De Were-Wolf

P.E. Master

Miss Nora Rock

Dr. Jekyll

Prof. Frankenstein

M. Quasimodo

Count Dracula

the Headmaster

son of Dracula

Hi!

The teachers were a well-qualified body of academics with more degrees than a thermometer.

The day began early with a brisk row on the bottomless lake of Transylvania, the Loch Mess. The instructor was Captain Blackbeard who sang sea-shanties and really wanted to be a pop singer.

Don't lose your dignity Nigel!

Physical fitness was very important, and so was the personal survival course.

Biology was taught by Professor Frankenstein. He was always trying to make something out of his pupils.

Chemistry was taken by Dr Jekyll. Sometimes by accident the lesson was taken by Mr Hyde, who seemed to be a supply teacher.

ROBIN HOOD, AND THE SHERIFF OF NOTTINGHAM

Robin Hood was an outlaw who earned an honest living robbing the rich, while his
merry men made merry in the Greenwood. Maid Marian was his girl-friend.
She believed in Women's Lib but had to wash the socks and cook the dinner.

After a day's hard fighting with the Sheriff's men, Robin Hood and his merry gang returned home where Maid Marian was waiting for them, burning something nice on the camp-fire.

The next day they had a go at the Sheriff's deer. The Sheriff didn't like this and led his gang of Normans after them.

When King Richard came back from his summer holidays, he gave Robin a knighthood in the New Year's honours list.

The dinner-lady was Miss Nora Rock, who cooked unforgettable dishes, as recommended by the Egg-on Ronay Guide.

The headmaster personally supervized school dinners. The pupils often had his favourite soup for starters, followed by Miss Nora's rock-cakes which were later used in the Geology lesson.

What a delightful young lady!

GOLDILOCKS AND THE THREE BEARS

RUPERT IS A WALLY!

UP THE GRIZZLIES!

BEARS RULE OK..!

In English they studied that gem of literature, 'Goldilocks and the Three Bears'. 'There was this cottage in the woods, all vandalized, and Goldilocks, who was a social worker, went to pay it a visit.

Inside she found three bowls of freshly vandalized food and she tasted them all because that's what she got paid for.

The first was Kitty-Kat, the second was Doggy-Dog, and the third was porridge which tasted all right if you like that sort of thing.

Then she found three chairs, all vandalized, and tried them out. The smallest was just right but it fell apart because she'd eaten all that porridge. Anyway, she went upstairs and saw these three beds. The first two were all vandalized but the third had an electric blanket, so she got in and had a good kip.

Then these three bears came back, having just vandalized the barbers.

WOT'S THIS THEN?

E.H?

OH NO!

The first one said, " 'Ere, some soft twit's been sittin' in me chair." The second one said, "Somebody's been sitting in *my* chair," because she'd got O level English. And the third one bawled his head off.

They saw the mess in the kitchen and rushed upstairs. The little one started bawling his head off again. Goldilocks woke up with all this racket going on and shouted, "I'm your friendly social worker."

WROOM... WROOM...

FULL SPEED AHEAD!

She dived out of the window, got on her BMX bike, and rode off like crazy with the three bears after her.

So she dived off this cliff-top and opened her parachute to make a soft landing. But the three bears went splat! at the bottom.

She landed next to this prince who was rehearsing for Jackanory.

She gave him a kiss. . . . but he wasn't amused.

Neither were the three bears and they never went vandalizing again.'

The End.

BIOLOGY! WE WATCHED A T.B.C. PROGRAMME ON ANIMAL BEHAVIOUR, CALLED:

STRAINING SLUGS THE GREENHOUSE WAY

For relaxation they watched a TBC programme presented by Mrs Barbara Greenhouse.

Night falls, the moon rises, the wolves howl, and the pupils lay down their weary heads. But young Dracula rises and looks for a bite of something. Can he resist the girls' necks door? Will it ever end . . . ?

Cook fell in love again. She wanted to marry the new PE master that Professor Frankenstein made. The music master was very shy. He always wore a mask and only came out at night to play the organ.